I0820605

CLEVELAND INDIANS

Sam Rhodes

Go to www.av2books.com, and enter this book's unique code.

BOOK CODE

AVV55638

AV² by Weigl brings you media enhanced books that support active learning.

AV² provides enriched content that supplements and complements this book. Weigl's AV² books strive to create inspired learning and engage young minds in a total learning experience.

Your AV² Media Enhanced books come alive with...

Audio
Listen to sections of the book read aloud.

Key Words
Study vocabulary, and complete a matching word activity.

Video
Watch informative video clips.

Quizzes
Test your knowledge.

Embedded Weblinks
Gain additional information for research.

Slide Show
View images and captions, and prepare a presentation.

Try This!
Complete activities and hands-on experiments.

... and much, much more!

Published by AV² by Weigl
350 5th Avenue, 59th Floor
New York, NY 10118
Website: www.av2books.com

Library of Congress Control Number: 2017963690

ISBN 978-1-4896-7980-2 (hardcover)
ISBN 978-1-4896-7981-9 (softcover)
ISBN 978-1-4896-7982-6 (multi-user eBook)

Printed in the United States of America in Brainerd, Minnesota
1 2 3 4 5 6 7 8 9 0 22 21 20 19 18

012018
120817

Project Coordinator: John Willis Designer: Nick Newton

The publisher acknowledges Getty Images, Alamy, and iStock as its primary image suppliers for this title.

Contents

The Indians' **first playoff** appearance was in 1920, when they won their first **World Series championship.**

GO, INDIANS!

When winter turns to spring, it is baseball season in Cleveland, Ohio. That is when the fans of the Cleveland Indians start getting excited. Wearing the team colors of red, white, and blue, they root for their team. Over their 117 seasons, the Cleveland Indians have made the playoffs 13 times and won the World Series twice. The Indians are always working hard to win again.

In 2017, the Indians took fans on a historic ride, winning 22 games in a row. It was the longest winning streak by any team in more than 100 years.

Pitcher Corey Kluber is known as "Klubot" because of his intense, robot-like concentration on the pitcher's mound. He often works with catcher Roberto Pérez.

Who Are the Indians?

Major League Baseball (MLB) is made up of the American League (AL) and the National League (NL). Within each league, there are three **divisions**. The Cleveland Indians play in the Central Division of the American League. After the regular season, the best teams in each division make the playoffs. The playoffs determine the league champions. The league champions then play in the World Series. The Indians have made six World Series appearances.

WHERE THEY CAME FROM

The Cleveland Indians joined the major leagues in 1901 as the Cleveland Blues. A year later, they changed their name to the Cleveland Broncos. The following year, looking for a fresh start, they changed their name again. They called themselves the Naps after their star second baseman, Napoléon "Nap" Lajoie. When Nap left in 1915, the team became the Cleveland Indians.

Roger Maris hit 14 home runs for the Indians in 1957. It was his first year in the major leagues.

José Ramírez is one of the best hitters in baseball. He was signed by Cleveland after filling in for another player at a Dominican Republic league game.

Who They Play

Every MLB team plays 162 games each season. Of those games, 76 are against other teams in their division. The other American League Central Division teams are the Minnesota Twins, the Kansas City Royals, the Chicago White Sox, and the Detroit Tigers. The Indians' biggest **rivals** are the Tigers. When Detroit and Cleveland play, the stadium gets loud!

In 2017, the Cleveland Indians had one of their **best regular season records** in team history, winning **102 games.**

Where They Play

The Indians play at Progressive Field in Cleveland. It was built in 1994. It replaced Cleveland Stadium, which was home to the Indians for nearly 50 years. Progressive Field seats more than 35,000 fans. Past the dugouts, there are special seats that are actually angled toward **home plate**. This gives fans a great view without having to twist around in their seats.

The playing area at Progressive Field is 105,000 square feet (9,800 square meters), 95,000 square feet (8,800 sq. m) of which is grass.

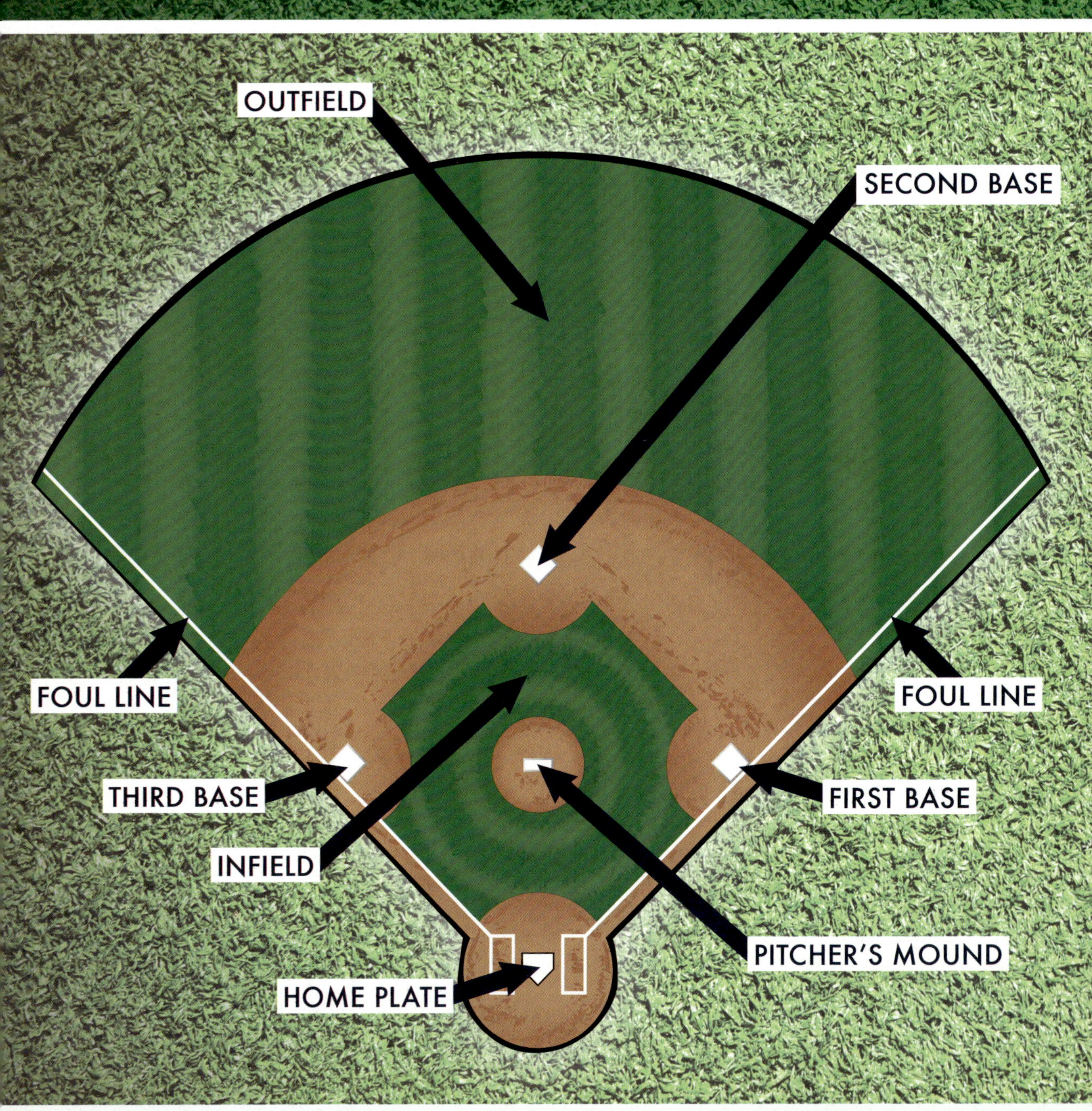
OUTFIELD
SECOND BASE
FOUL LINE
FOUL LINE
THIRD BASE
FIRST BASE
INFIELD
PITCHER'S MOUND
HOME PLATE

THE BASEBALL DIAMOND

Baseball games are played on a field called a diamond. Four bases form this diamond shape. The bases are 90 feet (27 meters) apart. The area around and between the bases is called the infield. At the center of the infield is the pitcher's mound. The grass area beyond the bases is called the outfield. White lines start at home plate and go toward the outfield. These are the foul lines. Baseballs hit outside these lines are out of play unless a fielder catches them. The outfield walls are about 300–450 feet (91–137 m) from home plate.

Big Days

The Cleveland Indians have had many extraordinary games. Here are three of their most celebrated victories:

1920: *In their first World Series, the Indians played the Brooklyn Robins, who later became the Dodgers. In Game 5, Indians right fielder Elmer Smith hit the first ever World Series* ***grand slam****. Then, second baseman Bill Wambsganss performed the first unassisted* ***triple play*** *in MLB history. Cleveland won both that game and the World Series.*

1948: *In Game 4 of the World Series, Indians center fielder Larry Doby hit a home run, and pitcher Steve Gromek held the Atlanta Braves' offense to a single run. The Indians took a commanding 3–1 series lead. They won the championship in Game 6.*

2016: *On July 1, the Indians and the Toronto Blue Jays played the longest game of 2016. It went 19 innings. The Indians' 2–1 win also broke the* ***franchise*** *record for longest winning streak. They broke this record again the following year.*

Shortstop Francisco Lindor won multiple awards for his performance with the Indians in 2016. It was his first full season playing professional baseball.

Second baseman Jason Kipnis had four hits and one run batted in during the 2017 postseason.

Tough Days

The Cleveland Indians have also been through tough times. Here are some of the worst moments in their franchise history:

1908: *The Cleveland Naps were competing with the Detroit Tigers for the American League* ***postseason*** *spot. The Naps went on a 10-game winning streak. However, it was not enough. They ended their 1908 season half a game behind the Tigers.*

1960: *Just before the 1960 season, Cleveland* ***traded*** *right fielder and fan favorite Rocky Colavito to the Detroit Tigers for outfielder Harvey Kuenn. Cleveland fans were heartbroken. Kuenn only played one season with the Indians. That trade sparked the 40-year* ***slump*** *called "The Curse of Rocky Colavito."*

2017: *In the final game of the American League Division Series, the Cleveland Indians faced the New York Yankees. The Indians played hard, but the Yankees won. The team returned to Cleveland, their hopes of winning their first World Series in 69 years dashed.*

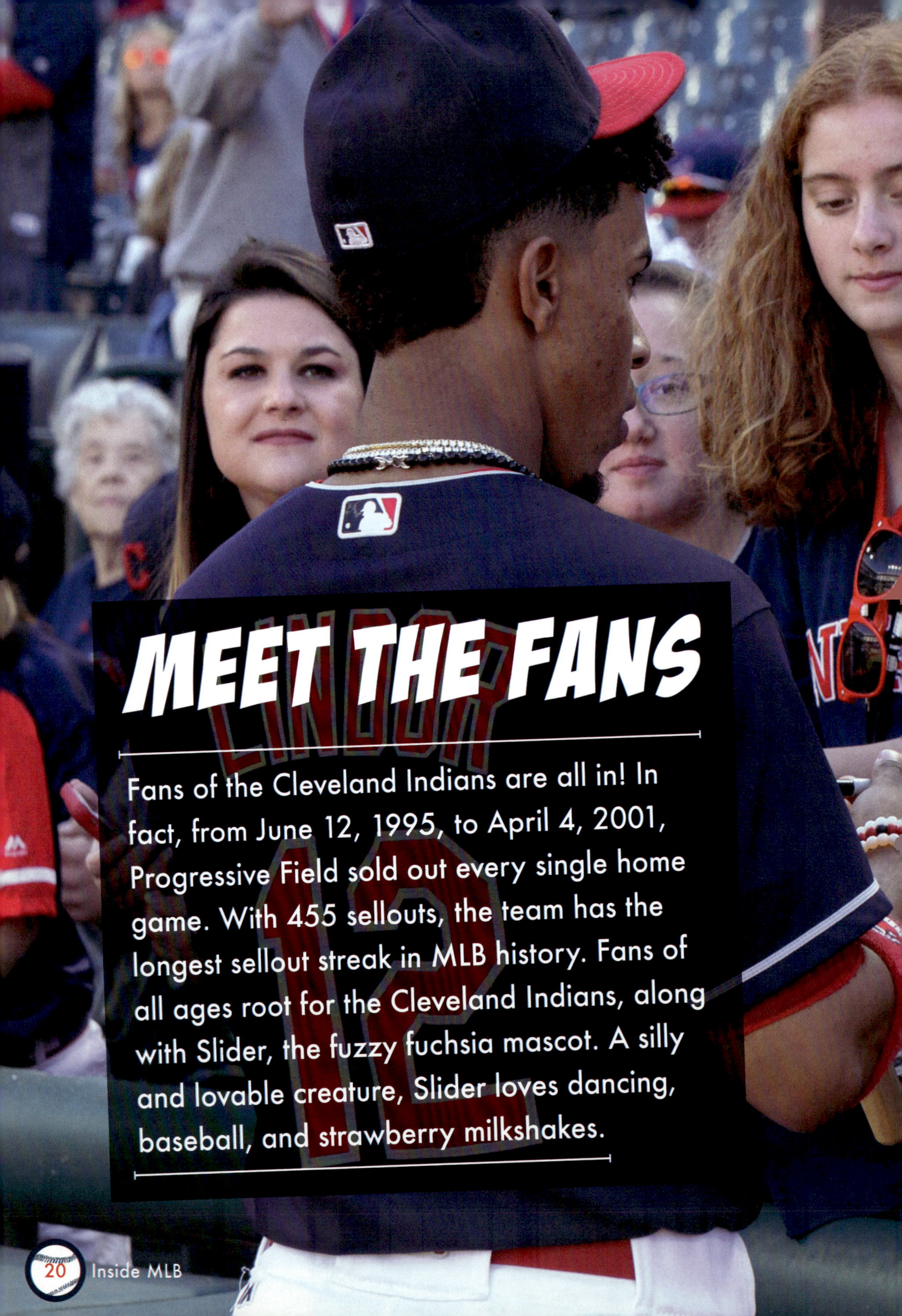

MEET THE FANS

Fans of the Cleveland Indians are all in! In fact, from June 12, 1995, to April 4, 2001, Progressive Field sold out every single home game. With 455 sellouts, the team has the longest sellout streak in MLB history. Fans of all ages root for the Cleveland Indians, along with Slider, the fuzzy fuchsia mascot. A silly and lovable creature, Slider loves dancing, baseball, and strawberry milkshakes.

Every year, Indians fans attend Tribe Fest, where they meet players, get autographs, and participate in baseball-themed activities.

Larry Doby, All-Star Player

Tris Speaker became an advisor for the Indians in 1947. He worked with Lou Boudreau, who was manager of the team from 1942 to 1950.

Heroes Then...

Fans of the Cleveland Indians have come to expect spectacular feats. Center fielder Tris Speaker played for Cleveland from 1916 to 1926. He has the sixth-best career batting average of any player in history. Napoléon "Nap" Lajoie was a star infielder. He led the league in hits, doubles, and batting average in 1901, 1904, and 1910. Pitcher Willie Mitchell threw whiffs, striking out many players, including Babe Ruth in 1914. Bob Feller, the 17-year-old prodigy, fired fastballs. As a rookie pitcher in 1936, he struck out 17 batters in one game. In 1947, Larry Doby was the first African American signed to the American League. Doby was a seven-time **All-Star Game** player who helped lead the Indians to their 1948 World Series win. Kenny Lofton was a stellar batter and baserunner. He led the American League in steals five years in a row, from 1992 to 1996.

Heroes Now...

Today, the Cleveland Indians are playing some of the best baseball in the club's history. They hope to win their first World Series in almost 70 years. Third baseman José Ramírez is cranking out doubles. He led the major leagues with 56 in 2017. A baseball team is only as good as its **bullpen**. Corey Kluber is setting a high bar with a 2.25 earned run average (ERA) in 2017. This 31-year-old pitcher is one of the best in the major leagues. Backing up Kluber is the relief pitcher Andrew Miller, a 12-year MLB veteran. Miller boasted a 1.44 ERA in 2017. The team's shortstop, Francisco Lindor, has been voted onto the All-Star team twice in his three-year MLB career. Big things are ahead for this young player and his team.

The present-day Indians are loaded with star players.

José Ramírez, Third Baseman

Corey Kluber, Pitcher

Francisco Lindor, Shortstop

Jason Kipnis, Second Baseman

GEARING UP

Baseball players all wear a team jersey and pants. They have to wear a team hat in the field and a helmet when batting. Take a look at Jason Kipnis and Yan Gomes to see some other parts of a baseball player's uniform.

Yan Gomes, Catcher

CATCHER'S MASK

CATCHER'S CHEST PROTECTOR

CATCHER'S MITT

CATCHER'S SHIN GUARD

SPORTS STATS

Here are some all-time career records for the Cleveland Indians. All of the stats are through the 2017 season.

A Major League baseball weighs about **5 ounces** (142 grams). It is **9 inches** (23 centimeters) around. A leather cover surrounds **hundreds** of feet of string. That string is wound around a small center of **rubber** and **cork**.

Home Runs

Jim Thome, **337**

Albert Belle, **242**

Runs Batted In

Howard Earl Averill, **1,084**

Jim Thome, **937**

Batting Average

"Shoeless" Joe Jackson, **.375**

Tris Speaker, **.354**

Stolen Bases

Kenny Lofton, **452**

Omar Vizquel, **279**

Wins by a Pitcher

Bob Feller, **266**

Mel Harder, **223**

Wins by a Manager

Lou Boudreau, **728**

Mike Hargrove, **721**

Earned Run Average

Addie Joss, **1.89**

Glenn Liebhardt, **2.17**

Quiz

1 How many times have the Indians made the playoffs?

2 How many times have the Indians won the World Series?

3 In what division do the Indians play?

4 Who are the Indians' biggest rivals?

5 In what year did the Indians first go to the World Series?

6 How long did the slump called "The Curse of Rocky Colavito" last?

7 Who was the first African American signed to the American League?

8 Who led the major leagues in doubles in 2017?

Answers

1. 13
2. Two
3. Central Division of the American League
4. The Detroit Tigers
5. 1920
6. 40 years
7. Larry Doby
8. José Ramirez

Key Words

All-Star Game: an annual midseason game in which the best players from the AL and NL play against each other

bullpen: the group of relief pitchers who can replace the starting pitcher

divisions: groups of teams that form one part of a professional sports league

franchise: a team that belongs to a professional sports league

grand slam: a home run when there are runners on all three bases

home plate: the base where a batter stands that a runner must touch to score a run

postseason: the time period after the regular season when additional games are played to determine a champion

rivals: teams that have a strong sense of competition with each other

slump: a period of doing poorly

traded: in sports, to have exchanged players between teams

triple play: a play made by the defensive team that puts three offensive runners out

Index

Log on to www.av2books.com

AV² by Weigl brings you media enhanced books that support active learning. Go to www.av2books.com, and enter the special code found on page 2 of this book. You will gain access to enriched and enhanced content that supplements and complements this book. Content includes video, audio, weblinks, quizzes, a slide show, and activities.

AV² Online Navigation

Audio
Listen to sections of the book read aloud.

Book Pages
AV² pages directly correspond to pages in the book.

Video
Watch informative video clips.

Embedded Weblinks
Gain additional information for research.

Key Words
Study vocabulary, and complete a matching word activity.

Try This!
Complete activities and hands-on experiments.

Quizzes
Test your knowledge.

Slide Show
View images and captions, and prepare a presentation.

AV² was built to bridge the gap between print and digital. We encourage you to tell us what you like and what you want to see in the future.

Sign up to be an AV² Ambassador at www.av2books.com/ambassador.

Due to the dynamic nature of the Internet, some of the URLs and activities provided as part of AV² by Weigl may have changed or ceased to exist. AV² by Weigl accepts no responsibility for any such changes. All media enhanced books are regularly monitored to update addresses and sites in a timely manner. Contact AV² by Weigl at 1-866-649-3445 or av2books@weigl.com with any questions, comments, or feedback.